Join the
MR.MEN & little miss
Club

Treat your child to membership of the popular Mr Men & Little Miss Club and see their delight when they receive a personal letter from Mr Happy and Little Miss Giggles, a club badge with their name on, and a superb Welcome Pack. And imagine how thrilled they'll be to receive a birthday card and Christmas card from the Mr Men and Little Misses!

Take a look at all of the great things in the Welcome Pack,

every one of them of superb quality (see box right). If it were on sale in the shops, the Pack alone would cost around £12.00. But a year's membership, including all of the other Club benefits, costs just £8.99 (plus 70p postage) with a 14 day money-back guarantee if you're not delighted.

To enrol your child please send your name, address and telephone number together with your child's full name, date of birth and address (including postcode)

and a cheque o ▮
(payable to Mr N
Mr Happy, Happ
142, Horsham RH
242727 to pay b

D1055899

The Welcome Pack:

✓ Membership card
✓ Personalized badge
✓ Club members' cassette with Mr Men stories and songs
✓ Copy of Mr Men magazine
✓ Mr Men sticker book
✓ Tiny Mr Men flock figure
✓ Mr Men notebook
✓ Mr Men bendy pen
✓ Mr Men eraser
✓ Mr Men book mark
✓ Mr Men key ring

Plus:

✓ Birthday card
✓ Christmas card
✓ Exclusive offers
✓ Easy way to order Mr Men & Little Miss merchandise

All for just £8.99! (plus 70p postage)

MORE SPECIAL OFFERS
FOR MR MEN AND LITTLE MISS READERS

In every Mr Men and Little Miss book like this one, and now in the Mr Men sticker and activity books, you will find a special token. Collect six tokens and we will send you a gift of your choice
Choose either a Mr Men or Little Miss poster, **or** a Mr Men or Little Miss **double sided** full colour bedroom door hanger.

Return this page **with six tokens per gift required** to:

Marketing Dept., MM / LM, World International Ltd.,
PO Box 7, Manchester, M19 2HD

Your name:_____ Age: _____

Address: _____

_____

_____Postcode: _____

Parent / Guardian Name (Please Print)_____

|— 100 mm —|

ENTRANCE FEE
3 SAUSAGES

250 mm

MR. GREEDY

Please tape a 20p coin to your request to cover part post and package cost

I enclose <u>six</u> tokens per gift, and 20p please send me:-

<u>Posters:-</u>   Mr Men Poster ☐   Little Miss Poster ☐

<u>Door Hangers</u> - Mr Nosey / Muddle ☐   Mr Greedy / Lazy ☐

20p   Mr Tickle / Grumpy ☐   Mr Slow / Busy ☐

Mr Messy / Quiet ☐   Mr Perfect / Forgetful ☐

L Miss Fun / Late ☐   L Miss Helpful / Tidy ☐

L Miss Busy / Brainy ☐   L Miss Star / Fun ☐

Stick 20p here please

Please Tick Appropriate Box

We may occasionally wish to advise you of other Mr Men gifts.
If you would rather we didn't please tick this box ☐

Collect six of these tokens
You will find one inside every
Mr Men and Little Miss book
which has this special offer.

1 TOKEN

Offer open to residents of UK, Channel Isles and Ireland only

MR. TICKLE
in a tangle

Original concept by Roger Hargreaves
Illustrated and written by Adam Hargreaves

MR MEN and LITTLE MISS™ & © 1998 Mrs Roger Hargreaves.
World International

Now, who does that extraordinarily long arm belong to?

Of course! Mr Tickle.

And Mr Tickle's long, long arms come in very handy.

They can reach kites caught in trees.

They can answer the phone when Mr Tickle is in the bath.

But, most importantly, they are splendidly perfect for tickling!

Tickling people round corners.

Tickling people through upstairs windows.

And even tickling people on the other side of letter-boxes!

However, there are days when those extraordinarily long arms are not so handy.

Days when they are nothing but a nuisance.

Days like last Monday.

Mr Tickle was lying in bed eating breakfast when he heard his garden gate open.

It was Mr Stamp, the postman.

Quick as a flash Mr Tickle sent one of his long arms down the stairs to tickle Mr Stamp.

Or, that is what he intended to do, but somehow or other, his arm got tangled up in the banisters.

Poor Mr Tickle!

It took him an hour to untangle his arm!

The letter Mr Stamp had delivered was an invitation from Mr Uppity, for lunch at the Grand Hotel.

Mr Tickle took the bus to town and sat on the upper deck.

Mr Tickle sent one of his long arms down the stairs to tickle the bus driver, but, somehow or other, the ticket inspector trod on his arm!

OUCH!

Mr Tickle arrived at the Grand Hotel and rushed through the revolving door.

Or rather he tried to, but, somehow or other, his arms caught in the door.

The fire brigade had to be called out to untangle his arms, by which time he had missed lunch.

Poor Mr Tickle.

No lunch, and even worse,

no tickles!

It was a very sad Mr Tickle who set off for home.

Suddenly he heard something.

He stopped. Somebody was approaching from around the corner.

Mr Tickle smiled to himself.

And sent both his arms around the corner to tickle that somebody.

But that somebody was Little Miss Naughty.

And she tied those extraordinarily long arms together in a knot!

When he got home Mr Tickle fell back into his armchair.

What a terrible day.

Not one tickle!

Suddenly there was a knock at the door.

It was Little Miss Tiny.

Mr Tickle stretched out one of his extraordinarily long arms.

Well, one tickle was better than none.

Even if it was only a tiny tickle!